RECKLESS CRUSADE

Patricia Wilson

Harlequin Books

TORONTO • NEW YORK • LONDON
AMSTERDAM • PARIS • SYDNEY • HAMBURG
STOCKHOLM • ATHENS • TOKYO • MILAN
MADRID • WARSAW • BUDAPEST • AUCKLAND

Special thanks and acknowledgment to Patricia Wilson

ISBN 0-373-15299-X

RECKLESS CRUSADE

First North American Edition 1995.

This edition Copyright © 1995 by Harlequin Enterprises B.V.

Copyright © 1992 by Patricia Wilson.

One

As she parked the car, Tamara Rawson's tawny eyes moved slowly along the lovely old buildings in Lancrest Mews to rest on the great hoarding that stood like an alien against the old hotel at the end. "Tysak Holdings." Boldly, it blazoned its message—"Danger. Reconstruction Work."

Tamara's lips tightened angrily. That infuriating message was the first thing she saw every day as she arrived to open her exclusive shop. The work was interfering with her business and she had dark suspicions about the future plans of Jason Tysak.

She hadn't even met him, but his name was pushed down her throat daily along with the dust, noise and general upheaval. She slammed the car door and marched across the small park to the mews. She had chosen this place very carefully when she opened Impressions.

It was not a shop really, but a salon, a chic and elegant one that catered for the rich matrons of the town and their clothes-conscious daughters. Now they were beginning to complain about the general lowering of the tone of the place. Tamara fumed daily but there wasn't a thing she could do about it.

Almost every penny she possessed was wrapped up in Impressions, and things had been going swimmingly until that hoarding had appeared, then the workmen who hammered, sawed, demolished and played a small but efficient transistor radio. They were very cheerful men, but boisterous.

Tamara had written letters of complaint, threatened legal action, but received nothing except polite regrets and promises of a speedy end to the torture. Nothing was happening speedily.

She let herself in and then stared grimly through the window. The place they called the park was actually a strip of land that stretched from the road to the cobbled path that fronted the four mews shops. It wasn't much wider than the lawn to a good-sized house but it was long and edged by beech trees.

There was an Edwardian elegance to Lancrest Mews, a little jewel in a busy town. Impressions was now a well-known place for beautiful clothes, Tamara's own creation. She had been a model since she was sixteen and when at almost twenty-four she had received a legacy she had risked everything to start here. Eric Simpson had a stylish hairdressing salon at the hotel end. Next door was Edwina Brown with a shop selling lingerie, swimwear, good costume jewellery, and other accessories. Tamara often bought for Edwina in London. At the other side

Kenneth Dennison had a shoe shop—Italian shoes and bags—and together they collected the carriage trade. Everything had been rosy until Jason Tysak had exploded on to the scene.

They had simply heard that someone had bought the Old Manor Hotel that stood high and slightly derelict at the end of the mews. None of them had been prepared for what followed. It was being extended and altered, and Tamara had dark suspicions that it would eventually extend itself to the whole of the mews!

Jason Tysak owned land and property all over the country—all over the world, in fact—so naturally they had never seen him. He certainly would not be sitting quietly in his temporary offices on Victoria Crescent. So far he had simply ignored the discreet shops in Lancrest Mews, but Tamara was sure he wanted them.

Tamara walked to the back of the shop and started sorting out the mail. She had been away on a buying trip in London for three days and things did pile up.

The sun slanted in at the window, catching all the fire of her hair, a honey-gold that was almost red. Shoulder-length and very wavy, it was caught back in a loose knot, revealing the fine bone-structure and wide amber eyes that had been such an asset in her modelling career.

Tamara turned with a smile as the door opened and her assistant stepped in. Janet Piper had been with her since the start.

"I'm back." Her cheerful greeting failed to bring an answering smile, and Tamara fancied that Janet was avoiding her eyes.

"Did you order anything spectacular?"

"A few special things. It just about completes our spring collection!" Tamara kept deliberately jaunty, but it was more than she could stand. "Janet, what is it? I know something's wrong."

"Oh, heavens! I thought I wouldn't dare tell you and now I'm sure." Janet knew her employer's temper. "Jason Tysak bought Lancrest Mews," she said in a rush. "Eric Simpson told me. He and Edwina have both had letters from the Tysak solicitors. I expect you'll get one too..."

"I expect so." Tamara walked back to the window. So, her suspicions had been correct! Their leases were just about ready for renewing but their landlord would no doubt pull down Lancrest Mews and extend that hotel over the whole area.

She went in to see Edwina.

"Oh, you're back! Get anything special?"

"I've been through this once with Janet," Tamara snapped. "What about the leases?"

"Tysak bought the whole works, darling." Edwina Brown, elegantly middle-aged, smiled wryly at her. "It's absolutely useless to get into a rage, Tamara. There's a lot of small print. The property can be sold at any time, providing the buyer offers reasonable compensation if he intends to turn us out. I've been on to the offices of Tysak Holdings and they assure me that there is no intention to turn us out permanently.''

"Permanently?'' Tamara's golden eyes narrowed.

"We have to move out for a few weeks at the end of this month while they sand-blast the fronts of the shops, to go with the new look of the Old Manor Hotel. Then we move back and everything goes on as normal—with a new landlord.''

"You believe all this?'' Tamara demanded. "Once out, we're out for good, I can tell you. When, for example, do we sign the new leases?''

"As far as we can tell, when we move back in. You see, we move out on the day our leases expire and in our temporary accommodation we'll be paying more rent than we do here. We don't want to take on two things at once, now, do we?''

How could anyone be so naïve? Tamara looked at her in disbelief and went round to the shoe shop to see Kenneth Dennison. He believed it too, and so did Eric. How could they be so blind?

With lunchtime over, business got under way again, but Tamara had to force a smile.

"Have you fixed a date for the fashion show, Tamara?'' One of the town's wealthiest matrons called in to ask about the annual event Impressions organised.

"Yes, Mrs. Prost. The same venue as usual too. One or two models are coming up from London, and then the local girls, of course. March twenty-seventh, at seven. All the new stock will be in by then.''

It wasn't until the door closed that the date rang a bell with Tamara. It was exactly four days before the leases ran out. There was always a rush of buying after the show, and this time they would be knee-deep in packing to move out. What could she do to outwit Tysak? He seemed to have them neatly tied up.

Tysak Holdings were at 63 Victoria Crescent, the biggest house on the road. Tamara pulled up outside and marched across to storm the ramparts. Just let them tell her she had no appointment! She didn't want to see the great Tysak personally—the old boy was probably sunning himself in the West Indies, his nurse handing out medicine. All she wanted was to state her case and send him a message of defiance—for now. The rest she would work out in secret.

She had to get past the young girl at reception first, and that was easy when she mentioned Lancrest Mews. It gave her entry to higher things—Mr. Tysak's personal assistant.

"You're very lucky, Miss Rawson," she said pleasantly. "Mr. Tysak is here at the moment."

"Himself?" Tamara asked. How would his poor old chest be standing up to an English winter?

"Oh, yes. We don't often have the pleasure," the disciple sighed. "He's been here for two days and he'll see you." She led the way to the inner sanctum.

"Miss Rawson," she breathed and then simply melted away, and Tamara was left standing in a high-ceilinged comfortable room all alone. There was a huge desk by the window and a high-backed leather chair turned to face outside.

Where on earth was he? Under the desk? Had the wily old man collapsed? Tamara stood there, wide-eyed and intrigued. And then as the chair slowly swung round, her mental pictures of a decrepit miser faded away as she found herself being regarded by dark, intent eyes.

"Please sit down, Miss Rawson." He stood politely and motioned her to a seat facing him. She could see at once that he would be a formidable foe. There was something about him that made a wave of confusion race over her.

Six feet two in his socks, he was handsome, with not one ounce of spare flesh on him. His cheekbones were high, classical, his eyes dark and spiked with black lashes that matched the dark, beautifully groomed hair. He was deeply tanned. In spite of the dark grey suit and pristine white shirt with silk tie, he looked dangerous, dramatically so; a noble savage.

"Geronimo," she whispered and the dark brows rose.

"I beg your pardon?"

"You surprised me," Tamara muttered, her cheeks beginning to glow a little. This was not the way to start a battle to the death.

"I was studying the street. A very beautiful crescent."

Probably wondering how many hotels he could shove into it. The suspicion brought Tamara back to earth.

"What can I do for you, Miss Rawson?" She didn't trust those gleaming eyes for one second. He couldn't be more than in his thirties, so how was it that he already owned millions? It had to be by sharp practices.

"You could leave town but I don't imagine it would help, the damage already having been done," she said.

"Your complaints have been passed on to me," he assured her. "If any of your—merchandise has been damaged then the company will replace it or recompense you. We have no wish to cause discomfort to any of the present tenants of Lancrest Mews."

Present tenants!

"There is dust, grit, noise and a general lowering of the tone of Lancrest Mews!" she bit out. "The mews shops are very special, Mr. Tysak."

"Yes." His dark eyes were on her furious face. "That's why I bought them. They need a fair bit of work, but it will be worthwhile."

"For whom? I know perfectly well you intend to allow that monstrosity to encroach on Lancrest Mews."

"You mean the hotel? Have you seen the plans, Miss Rawson?"

"I have, but I don't believe it for a moment. I know what you're going to do. You'll keep the façade, the shops too, and then expand behind until the hotel takes up the whole mews. The fronts of the mews shops will probably end up as the windows of some hideous lounge in the hotel."

"You're no architect, Miss Rawson, I can see that." He sounded amused, condescendingly so. "Let me explain it to you." He stood smoothly, but Tamara too was on her feet.

"Don't bother, because I wouldn't believe a word. I intend to expose you, so get ready for action."

"If it amuses you, Miss Rawson," he agreed politely. "But I own the property, and I have planning permission."

"And that wasn't obtained in a day either," Tamara fumed. "No doubt you intend to put in new plans when we've all been evicted. Well, you won't get them through."

"I'm an irresistible force," he assured her coldly.

"And I am an immovable object. Anyway, until the end of March we're quite safe."

"I'm not sure that a girl like you can bank on safety." His glance ran over her very comprehensively, deliberately insolent, a very male speculation in his eyes. She had the shocking feeling that he was slowly undressing her, and then he pressed a button on his desk.

"Show Miss Rawson out, Miss Phillips," he murmured, "and give her a copy of the plans for Lancrest Mews." He sounded utterly bored and dismissive.

"No, thank you! They're carved across my heart!" Tamara marched out, infuriated when just before the door swished shut she heard low dark laughter. He thought he held all the cards. Power, wealth and sexual superiority. He would find out. "He who laughs last laughs longest," she muttered as she got into her car and drove away.

It was too late to go back to the shop and she went straight home to her flat. It was the entire ground floor of a large Victorian house at the edge of town, and she had done all the interior designing herself. Everything was pastel shades, from walls to carpets to the oatmeal-coloured suite. The colour came in curtains, cushions and the good prints on the walls. The huge one over the fireplace had been a present from her agent. It depicted London with St. Paul's in the background and, looking at it now, she wished herself back there.

Quick-tempered or not, she had no wish to fight anyone. Scenes were not her style and neither was battle, but she hated injustice. She made herself a cup of tea and then settled down to the telephone.

"Hello, Mum? I'm back." She found herself smiling when she heard her mother's voice, imagining her kind, pretty face and feeling she was safely back at home.

"Where's Dad?" Tamara asked.

"Out, Tamara. Where else? He has his rounds to do before evening surgery." Her father was a doctor in a Cumbrian village. She wished she were home now. She wanted to tell them both about Jason Tysak, to see her father nod in agreement at what she had decided to do, to see her mother's outrage at high-handed ways. It was no use; she didn't have time to drive up there now.

As soon as she put the phone down it rang. It was Roger Hart, editor of the local paper and her part-time boyfriend.

"Hello! You're back, then? Have dinner with me tonight."

"I'd love to," Tamara accepted. "I've got a lot to say."

"Yes can be said with little time taken," he murmured seductively. "I'll pick you up at seven-thirty."

He rang off then. It was Roger who called himself her part-time boyfriend and it worried her sometimes. He was just a friend, a good one but still nothing more than that.

Even so, she was always pleased to see him and this evening more so than ever. She trusted him completely and as they settled down to their meal in a quiet local restaurant she leaned forward and prepared to enlighten him about her plans and gain whatever aid she could.

"You know about the fate of Lancrest Mews, I suppose?"

"What fate?" He was instantly alert.

"In my opinion, Jason Tysak is about to incorporate the whole of the mews into the Old Manor Hotel."

"Not possible." Roger shook his head. "I've seen the plans. They're at the council offices. We printed the planning request and the permission. Nobody objected."

"Of course they didn't!" Tamara said indignantly. "Who would object to the Old Manor Hotel being restored? The place was an eyesore."

"Well, you've objected daily since work began," Roger stated with an amused glance. "So have your customers. I've never had so many 'Letters to the Editor.' "

"I object to the uncouth way they're going about it. But one day it will be finished. Now, however, Jason Tysak is going to extend it along the mews."

"He can't, love," Roger explained. "There's an order on those places. They're a true Edwardian façade."

"But what about the backs?" Tamara asked. "The backs of the buildings are a medley of indiscriminate additions."

"I agree. But what's your point?" Roger asked.

"If I were Jason Tysak," Tamara continued, "I would keep the façade of Lancrest Mews and sweep the hotel into an extension around the back. I would call it Lancrest Mews Hotel, Edwardian elegance for the discerning. I would boot out the present tenants and have the park as a very nice frontage to the hotel."

"A deadly plan," Roger agreed, nodding sagely. "However, nothing like that is in the wind."

"Then I'll give you some news," Tamara offered. "Jason Tysak has bought Lancrest Mews. We all move out at the end of March, supposedly for a brief time until the fronts are sand-blasted. No date set for the renewal of the leases. Now what about the deadly plan?"

Roger regarded her intently. She could see she had him hooked. If there was anything to find out, Roger would find it.

Two

Roger arrived at the shop next day just after eleven, and Tamara knew he was hunting news. Tysak's architect was out at the back with some other men, and Roger sauntered round to begin an easygoing conversation. Tamara's excitement grew the longer Roger stayed. She would know for sure after this.

"Well? What did you find out?" She pounced on him as he came back in.

"Nothing. Either the whole firm has been told to clam up or I'm losing my touch. But I have the urge to write an article. Let's flush them out, shall we?" He grinned at Tamara and she almost rubbed her hands in glee.

Later in the day she had the chance for more action, starting with her first customer after lunch— Mrs. Prost.

"How you're putting up with this noise and dust I can't think, Tamara," she commiserated.

"Well, it won't concern us for much longer," Tamara confided. "At the end of March we're all moving out. I just don't know how we'll cope with the after-fashion-show rush.''

"Moving out? What do you mean?" Duly startled, Mrs. Prost fixed Tamara with a disapproving eye.

"Why, didn't you know?" Tamara asked. "The leases expire at the end of March and Tysak Holdings have bought the mews. Of course, we're being offered temporary accommodation. Those new shops in Charles Street.''

"Charles Street! My dear, it's so down-market. How long do you expect to be there?''

"Ah!" Tamara said. "We're *supposed* to be coming back here after a while, but since Tysak Holdings develop property..."

"But this is Edwardian property. Surely the council..."

"Only the façade has an order on it," Tamara said. "Who knows about the back?"

Mrs. Prost was too stunned to reply. She picked up her box and simply walked out, shattered by the blow, and Tamara knew she would not have to do any more spreading of the word. Mrs. Prost was a gossip *par excellence*. Things were moving.

On Friday, Tamara read Roger's article eagerly. The heading was eye-catching—"Mystery of the Mews."

This paper understands that the refined and lovely Lancrest Mews has been bought up by

Tysak Holdings. The council are very coy about the whole matter, and it does spring to mind that the Old Manor Hotel, another Tysak property, stands at the end of the mews. A coincidence? Perhaps it is time that Tysak Holdings set a few minds to rest and stated their aims.

It went on in like vein, and Tamara read every word earnestly. It would inspire her small army of supporters, infuriate Jason Tysak and maybe, just maybe, he would back off and leave things alone.

All day it rained miserably. The park was almost invisible as water ran down the windows, and long before closing time it was very dark. Tamara let Janet go early to catch her bus.

Tamara started cashing up and doing the stock list, but she hadn't got far when the sound of the bell sent her back into the shop.

Her heart did a very wild swing as she saw Jason Tysak in the doorway. He looked even taller in a white belted raincoat with the collar turned up. His shoulders were wet and his dark hair gleamed with water.

He was furious, and Tamara had no doubt why, even without the copy of the local paper, wet and folded, in his hand. He slammed the door and advanced menacingly.

"Is this your doing?" he grated.

"I'm not a journalist," Tamara assured him.

"No," he rasped, "you're a trouble-maker, and a very ill-informed one! My phone has been ringing all day about this article. I haven't forgotten your threats, Miss Rawson."

"People have a right to know what's going on in their own town, under their very noses!"

"*Nothing* is going on! Let me remind you that I got you the temporary accommodation. I have no obligation to rehouse any of you. What then, Miss Rawson? Where do you go from here?"

"Straight to the paper," Tamara assured him tartly. "Threats! That sounds like good copy to me."

"Keep out from under my feet!" he warned angrily, his eyes flashing. "So far it's just a minor irritation. Keep this up and you have a battle on your hands!"

The next act in the drama left Tamara wondering just what she had started. The local paper also did a lot of printing, and Roger rang to ask if she had seen the leaflets.

"What leaflets?" Instantly she was wary.

"About the mews." Roger gave a sarcastic little laugh. "I know you got someone to order them. No need to be coy with me."

"I'm not being coy!" Tamara stated. "As to leaflets, you'd better tell me."

"I'll read one out. Heading, 'Our Edwardian Heritage.' Substance,

Do we intend to ignore the fact that once
again developers are changing the face of our
town? Lancrest Mews is at risk at this moment,
and where will this sort of thing stop? Write to
your council and demand explanations.

Et cetera, et cetera.''

The longer it went on, the more glowing became
Tamara's cheeks.

"I know your name isn't on the order form," he
murmured in amusement, "but it's just your fighting style. Want to tell me about it?"

"I honestly don't know a thing about it," Tamara got out in a rush of embarrassment. It was just
such an action she had wanted, but, after facing Jason Tysak the week before, she was not now so very
sure of her ground. He would put it down to her too,
and she wasn't altogether certain about what he
would do. "Who *ordered* the leaflets?" Tamara demanded.

"Mrs. Prost, on behalf of the committee to save
the mews," Roger informed her. "There's a whole
bevy of ladies with their names printed here, and
you're an honorary member, in brackets."

"I don't know anything about it!" Tamara protested.

"Be that as it may, sweetie," Roger murmured,
"we printed two thousand, and they've been collected. It was a rush job."

Tamara stared out at the dismal scene from the back of the shop as Roger rang off. It had rained all weekend, and today there had been no architect around, no surveyor. She dreaded the thought of Jason Tysak's coming round.

She walked into the shop with a forced smile and faced the two remaining customers, both heading into the changing-rooms.

"It's a terrible night," one said. "The river's up again."

"Well, we're safe here," Tamara consoled. But tonight she would leave when Janet left.

Jason Tysak walked in two seconds later, and he slammed a leaflet down on the counter.

"This, I take it, is your declaration of war!" he rasped. "Right now a copy of this leaflet is with my solicitor. If I can find anything to get you on I'll make you sorry you ever *saw* Lancrest Mews. And you can all forget the temporary accommodation!"

"In the first place, I had nothing to do with those leaflets," Tamara stormed. "I only just found out about them myself. In the second place, even if I had, it's got nothing to do with the others in the mews. You can't punish them because of me!"

"You'll find I can do exactly as I like, Miss Rawson!"

"It's not fair!" She glared up at him.

"*Fair*! What do you know about being fair?" He actually roared, and Tamara was suddenly aware that there were two customers in the changing cubicles and Janet, standing wide-eyed over at the side. She grabbed his arm, quaking at the feel of taut, angry muscles.

"You can't make a scene here, Mr. Tysak! This is my establishment and I must ask you to leave."

She was so anxious to get him out of the shop that she kept on going towards the door, her impetus moving them both forward. As she opened it to the pouring rain, his expression of astonished ferocity made her pause and with that, he took control, stepping out into the rain with her and closing the door.

"I would very much like to wring your beautiful neck!" he informed her. "On the other hand, there's a good chance that your brain is only loosely attached to your body, so we'll try another lesson."

The small, hard awning over the door had been sheltering them, but now he thrust Tamara out into the rain, his arm lashing round her waist, his other hand tilting her head until the full force of the cold rain poured into her upturned face.

She had to close her eyes as the rain made her gasp for breath and then it was cut off as his dark head bent over hers, and her gasp turned to violent shock as his hard lips closed over hers in a devastating kiss that momentarily made her feel faint.

It only lasted for a second but it seemed that she was drowning all over again, this time in the taste of a furious and powerful male animal.

"Now you know not to play outside your league," he grated, his dark eyes burning into her. "Tomorrow you'll be hearing more from me."

"I think you'll be hearing from my solicitor," she managed shakily. "I've just been physically assaulted in front of my own premises with at least one witness."

"Three witnesses actually," he growled. "What they saw was an admirer kissing you, Miss Rawson."

"How dare you? They know what they saw, and when I get back in they'll be in no doubt."

"Well, then, we'll have to give them doubts, won't we?" he said and before she could move Tamara found herself back in those strong, hateful arms and now he turned her towards the light as his mouth came down on hers. This time he kissed her slowly and sensuously until she murmured anxiously against his lips.

A quite terrifying burst of feeling hit her deep inside, somewhere between her stomach and her legs. It was a feeling she had never known and it overwhelmed her. Somehow he knew and drew her closer, as all the fight went out of her. It was an almost brutal shock when he lifted his head and moved slightly away.

"Now tell them," he advised sardonically. "*Two* attacks—but the victim was quite obviously willing."

"Nobody will believe it," Tamara gasped, her mouth still burning. She seemed to be pulsing with feeling, her breasts tight and swollen. "They know me."

"They'll know you better tomorrow," he promised softly. "You're the girl who got everyone else tossed out with no temporary accommodation. Notorious is the word that will fit you. Go inside, my dear Miss Rawson. You're quite wet."

"You just might have to apologise, darling," Susan Rawson pointed out. "It might be the only way to save your accommodation." Tamara had rung her mother to tell her that part of the story.

"I will not apologise to that—that heathen! In any case," she added, "he wouldn't listen."

"How do you know?"

"Because he's a savage with pots of money," Tamara said lamely. She had not told her mother about this evening's final happenings.

Next day there were closed signs on all four shops and Tamara walked into a heated discussion between friends.

"Why are we all closed?"

Impressions' elegant chairs were occupied by her neighbours, and Janet stood anxiously by.

"We all had telephone calls earlier this morning, Tamara," Edwina Brown said. "Tysak Holdings threaten to refuse temporary accommodation unless we can control you."

"What?" Tamara stared at them, outraged.

"You'll have to apologise," Kenneth Dennison stated. "You may be able to afford to wait this out, but I can't."

"Neither can I," Tamara seethed. "What makes you think we'll be back here finally, in any case?"

"Tysak Holdings assured us that—"

"Tysak Holdings is Jason Tysak!" Tamara fumed.

"I'm beginning to think there's something between you and Tysak," Edwina mused.

"There is," Tamara snapped. "It's called bitter enmity."

"Well," Kenneth said, "You started this, Tamara. I for one will leave it to your conscience."

They walked out together, although Eric did stop to pat Tamara's arm.

"Open up for business, Janet," she ordered bleakly and got straight on the phone. Her mother was right. She would have to apologise.

When she finally got through to Jason Tysak, he stated coldly, "You may apologise to my face, Miss Rawson. I expect to see you in my office in fifteen minutes." He just put the phone down, and Tamara stared at it grimly, her golden eyes narrowed. He intended to see her squirm. Well, she wouldn't!

He was contemplating the crescent again but this time he was standing, hands in his pockets, his jacket slung over the back of his chair, and he turned slowly as she came into the room, closing the door behind her.

He stood and looked at her steadily, a frown on his dark face as he noticed the wings of defiant colour across her cheeks. He didn't need to be told how she felt—it was all there in her tawny eyes.

"There's nothing subdued about you, is there, Miss Rawson? I imagined you were here to apologise, but you seem more angry than ever."

"Did you expect me to be pleased?" Tamara asked. "You know that I'm here under duress. Obviously you're not used to people who fight back."

"There was never anything to fight about, Miss Rawson," he pointed out grimly. "You have brought this whole thing down to an undignified public skirmish. You have also reduced me to acting the part of a chauvinistic male."

Tamara's face flushed more wildly.

"You did all that by yourself. Nobody has ever treated me like that before!"

"Perhaps that's what's wrong," he muttered. "You've been spoiled. Being beautiful is not a passport to behaving exactly as you like. Perhaps this little episode will help to straighten you out."

"I can do without the moral lecture. I came to apologise."

"Then begin, Miss Rawson. And please sit down."

"I prefer to stand." Tamara stared at him with great dislike, although it was difficult to juggle her feelings.

"I—I'm sorry that I infuriated you," she said rapidly, her carefully rehearsed little speech having fled now that she was actually facing him. His dark brows rose ironically.

"My fury is a little aside we can forget about," he assured her. "It is the actual hard damage you're here to atone for, Miss Rawson. Let me point out that a business like mine requires a great deal of good will. When I buy land and put in plans a certain standard is expected. If word of this sordid little battle spreads, Tysak Holdings will be looked at with a very suspicious eye by all planners. It is not merely your irritating presence that annoys. I have to think of my firm. So a small, meek and quite unwilling apology will not do. I want something of more substance."

"I—I'll send you a letter," Tamara said.

"You will send a letter of apology to the paper," he insisted. "You made this a public battle. You will apologise in public. I want to see it in this week's edition—arrange it with your boyfriend."

"*What*?" Tamara jumped up and stared at him wildly. "I can't do that! Roger . . . the editor will be furious. He's written about this too. Why aren't you going after him?"

"I rely on you to take the wind out of his sails, Miss Rawson. You started this. You will finish it."

"And what about my customers? They're right behind me in this. They—they even started a committee."

"They can disband it," he pointed out.

"I'll lose their custom. I rely on them."

"You have an exclusive establishment. If they want the clothes they'll come back. When you're a little older and a little wiser you'll learn to think before you act."

"Did you think before you acted the other night?" Tamara enquired furiously.

"No. I acted on impulse. Most unusual for me. You infuriated me. You've probably been kissed by some frustrated male before, however, or don't you leave them frustrated?"

"I did not come here to be insulted!" Tamara snapped.

"No. As I've told you, I want a written apology in this week's paper. Otherwise you all lose your temporary accommodation."

"It was never going to be temporary," Tamara said bleakly. "I know you intend to build on the mews."

"I do," he said. "I intend to amalgamate everything into one very attractive unit dominated by the hotel."

"You're a snake in the grass!" Tamara glared at him. All her forebodings had come to pass.

She was barely back in the shop when Edwina came rushing round.

"Who's minding your store?" Tamara asked sourly. But Edwina was in a placatory mood.

"I know you didn't want to do this, Tamara," she said, "but it's our livelihood. So do we keep our temporary accommodation?"

"When I've apologised."

"But I thought that's where you'd been?"

"Tysak wants a written apology in the next edition of the paper. He intends to humiliate me."

"Oh, Tamara! We never meant this to happen. You didn't put the notices around, after all."

Janet was squirming, and it became obvious as to why when Mrs. Prost stepped out of a changing-room, half in and half out of a sugar-pink evening gown.

"My dear, I couldn't help overhearing. This is disgraceful! We'll not allow you to be humiliated like this. He's browbeaten you!" she went on furiously. "It can be done so easily to the young." She stepped back into the changing-room, and in seconds handed out the gown. "Put this on my account, Janet," she ordered, standing there in her slip. "I'll collect it later. I have things to do." As she slid into her suit, she told them, "there's a public meeting tomorrow night at the Bounty Rooms. I did intend to invite you all, but I can see it wouldn't be a good idea. Stay out of the limelight, Tamara, and leave everything to me."

"Oh, I don't think . . . It wouldn't be wise . . ." Tamara began anxiously, but Mrs. Prost was in full cry.

"This is town business," she reminded them all firmly, "a civic affair. Many important people are quite outraged. I'll keep you informed." She swept out, determination written across her face, and Tamara sank into a chair.

"He'll think I did it," she said worriedly. "He'll think I came straight back and went to Mrs. Prost and gang. You can't blame me for this, Edwina. A steamroller couldn't stop that woman."

"What to do now?" Edwina asked.

"There's only one thing to do," Tamara said. "I'll have to let him know. If we're to stand any chance at all I've got to warn him."

When Janet had gone to lunch, she picked up the phone with a great deal of reluctance.   "I sincerely hope you're not about to tell me you've changed your mind about that letter," Tysak said.

"No. I have news for you." Tamara struggled to control her nerves. "I—I just found out that there's a meeting tomorrow night at the Bounty Rooms," she said anxiously. "The—the committee have called it and it's a public meeting about—"

"I have no doubts at all what it's about!" he assured her caustically. "When did you change sides? Better think about that. I might lose this battle. Place your bets very carefully, Miss Rawson. Being disloyal is a tricky business, whoever wins."

"I'm not being disloyal!" Tamara protested.

"Forget about that letter to the paper," he said suddenly and she had to admit that scared her a little. She was out of her league, as he had said.

"Are you going to toss us all out?" she asked.

"Wait and see," he rasped. "Let's hope the suspense doesn't kill you."

He put the phone down and Tamara looked at herself in the mirror, astonished at her shaken appearance.

They all got letters the next day, delivered by hand from the Tysak solicitors, and the news prompted an instant meeting.

"We're to stay here. No need to move at all," Eric stated. "Apologies for any anxiety caused."

"What do you think?" Edwina asked Tamara. "You know him."

"I've decided not to think at all in future," Tamara assured her. "As to knowing him, I don't. He's the quick brown fox." Inside she knew he was more the big bad wolf but there was no need to wipe the happy looks from their faces.

"We'll have to play it by ear," she suggested. "Let's forget it for now, shall we? There's the fashion show to organise, after all."

"I hope he doesn't change his mind after tonight's meeting," Edwina muttered worriedly as the others left.

It was difficult to sleep that night, and next day as the phone rang Tamara actually jumped.

"Thought I would just set your mind at rest, dear," Mrs. Prost said. "You're all to stay there. I expect he'll let you know."

"Did he go to the meeting?" Tamara asked quickly.

"His solicitor," Mrs. Prost said grimly. "Of course, this is not the end of the matter. We'll be keeping an eye on things. You did say that he was probably going to take the whole of Lancrest Mews. I haven't forgotten."

Well, it didn't matter anyway, Tamara mused as she put the phone down. She would wait a while and see what happened.

The phone rang again as she was going back into the shop. "There will be workmen round today," Jason Tysak said. "Please inform the others. I will also be there this afternoon with my architect. I need to see the upper storeys of the mews."

When he came in she stared at him in a mesmerised way that brought a quirk to his lips and a dancing light to the dark eyes.

"My architect, Miss Rawson," he murmured, indicating his companion. "You'll be seeing a fair bit of each other, so you'd better get on good terms."

She was still staring as her hand was shaken vigorously by a fair-haired young man with very studious-looking spectacles.

"Er—how do you do?" she muttered. "Do you need any help?"

"Just show us how to get upstairs," Jason said. "We don't want to get in your way."

"There's a door in the back," she offered.

"Do you store things up there?" he asked quietly, stalking along behind her and making her skin go hot.

"No. I've never even been up there."

Janet had retreated to the very front of the shop. As soon as they had the door unlocked she sprang into action. "I'll sort out the cups," she said. "We must offer them a coffee."

"We must do no such thing!" Tamara snapped. "We want them out of here fast."

"Diplomacy!" Janet whispered.

"He's false and dangerous. Beware," Tamara warned. Janet just shot her a wary look and disappeared into the back.

There was a good deal of banging from aloft and not one customer came in. Tamara went to warn Edwina of approaching invasion and left her shaken. It was getting to be like a farce, she decided, slipping back into the shop as the two men encountered Janet with cups at the ready.

"That's very kind of you," Tysak beamed at her. "Janet, isn't it?"

He strolled over to stand by the window, tall and dark at her side, as Tamara looked out at the park, trying to ignore him.

"Stop sulking," he murmured. "You've not lost entirely. You might even approve of what I'm going to do."

"You mean, the part where you refuse to renew the leases?"

"I think I'll let you worry about that for a little while," he said. "You deserve it. Are they all trembling too?"

"I haven't told them about your plans," Tamara snapped. "They couldn't take the shock. And I'm not trembling!"

"Really?" He looked down at her hands and she put them hastily into the pockets of her silk skirt, feeling hot and cold all over when he gave a low, dark laugh.

"Why were you looking at the windows?" Tamara asked.

"We'll have to make some alterations." He was grinning to himself, she noted. "I've been considering your complaints. Dust and noise. You'll have workmen here shortly to double-glaze for you and put some excluders on the doors."

"It will mean emptying the windows!" Tamara gasped. "It takes hours to do them."

"You can't have it all ways," he pointed out. "I had intended to do all this while you were in your other accommodation but..." He looked down at her steadily and she bit her lip in deep vexation.

Three

With the fashion show looming ever closer, Tamara settled down to a good deal of organising. The spring clothes were delivered, and that too brought extra work.

The alterations had been a nuisance, especially when the men informed her that it would take a little longer because of the long bow windows. They had also endured a time of deep chill as the excluders were fitted to the doors. It was all over now, though. There was less noise and no dust at all.

The windows had been dressed again and everything cleaned up. She had half expected a visit from Jason to view the work, but obviously he did not sink to inspecting minutiae, and so far nothing was happening in the upper storeys of Lancrest Mews. Peace of a sort reigned.

The fashion show was held each year at the local secondary school, a new building in well-kept grounds with plenty of parking space. The auditorium stage was pretty much perfect, and the local carpenter had made a catwalk that stretched out into the audience.

The show was always packed and this year was no exception, in spite of the wet weather. Tamara peeped out from behind the curtains and cast an eye over the murmuring audience. Plenty of clients there.

She and Janet had been here since early afternoon, putting the clothes out for each model. Edwina had come along later with her own things as had Kenneth Dennison. The girls had all been given free hair-dos by Eric and it looked like being a very professional, glittering show.

There was only one person missing, and Tamara's head rose as Mrs. Prost came in, quite flustered and alone. Not again!

"Oh, Tamara! I'm so sorry. Gillian has one of her headaches. She just can't make it tonight."

"Why do we bother with that wretched girl?" Janet muttered. "This is the second time she's let us down in three shows. Twice in a row too. She did this at the autumn show, and I know perfectly well it was because of that party at the tennis club."

"We'll have to manage," Tamara said. Mrs. Prost actually looked uncomfortable and it served her right. She knew perfectly well how unreliable her daughter was.

"This is the very last time," she murmured to Janet.

"I'll keep you to that. Jane will have to wear a size twelve. I'll pin her into it."

It was all pretty hectic, but when the music struck up they were all ready, the local girls being hushed severely by Edwina, the professional models enjoying themselves enormously. Tamara peeped once again through the curtains, watching the girls. Pretty good!

Suddenly her face froze. He was there, right by the edge of the catwalk, a woman with him. What was Jason doing here? For a wild minute she thought he had come to get his own back, to wreck her show, but common sense told her he would do no such thing.

"This is probably the best show we've done yet!" Janet exclaimed, rushing in to help her girl change fast. "What's next?"

"The pink suit." Tamara glanced at her clipboard.

"What about the swimwear in the finale?" Edwina asked in a frosty voice. "How can anyone double up for Miss Gillian Prost then? Do I go out and just hold it up?"

She was very annoyed, and Tamara could see another battle beginning as Mrs. Prost's face reddened further.

"Why don't you wear it, Tamara?" one of the dressers said.

"I'm not a model."

"You could walk back into a job in London any time you wanted," one of the London girls said wryly.

Tamara would have said yes with no further thought, but Jason was out there, that woman with him. It was thinking of the woman that brought her out of her nervous dither.

"Fine. I'll do it." It sounded like somebody else's voice, and later she wished it had been.

It was to be the very last item. Gillian was to enter as all the other models stood at the side and posed. The bathing suit was eye-catching in more ways than one. Like the matching wrap, it was a swirl of vivid colour overlaid with silver roses, not something she would have chosen herself. Without the wrap it was clinging, brief and high-legged.

Tamara lingered in the changing-room, her heart beating alarmingly. This was where she made a spectacle of herself.

The London models whistled and grinned when she stepped out, and Tamara found herself smiling. She had enjoyed modelling. She should never have tried her hand at business. It gave her something to ponder as she waited for the music.

She stepped out slowly on cue, taking up the beat, and just for a moment she forgot that dark eyes would be watching her. She was back in the big fashion shows, the excitement of an audience, the music and the make-up all combining to send her far back into the past.

To say they were stunned was putting it mildly. Of course, they all recognised her. She was well known in town—for her smart clothes, her quiet demure air. Now they were looking at something else. Her sheer beauty, her professional gloss, and her deliberately sexy walk stunned them.

In the middle of the catwalk she discarded the wrap with a swirl of movement, and then the applause came *and* the whistles. She was enjoying herself, playing a game. She followed it through to the end, coming back to the stage where the models were applauding too and then walking back, swinging the gauzy wrap.

Roger stood up in the audience, clapping wildly and she flashed him a very professional smile. It was only when she looked at Jason that the devil really got into her at the look on his face. Far from being captivated, he disapproved! She paused deliberately and winked at him openly and slowly. That almost brought the house down.

She was glad to get off then. In fact, she just wanted to lock the cubicle door and recover. The wink had been just too much and she knew it. She also knew that Jason would be at the party afterwards. He had been sitting in a reserved seat. Those seats paid more and they also paid for the party. It was all for charity. She tried to hang back, but it was impossible.

"Get over to the party," the helpers insisted. "We'll clear up."

The private room at the King's Head was already crowded when Tamara arrived, and she tried to slip in unnoticed. But she couldn't have been more visible if she had come in the swimsuit.

It was a relief to chat to people she knew, and Roger soon joined them. "So that's what you did in London!" he murmured, slipping his arm round her. "It's a good job you're already my girl or I would be anxious."

It was a bit difficult to remind him that she was no such thing, so she had to smile sweetly and put up with it. And she hadn't done swimwear and undies in London. She had always refused.

Jason, she noted, was at the other side of the room, ignoring her. His lady-love was in black and it suited her enormously, a silk wrap-over dress that cleverly clung to her figure. She looked like someone who would travel the world with ease. Her jewellery was fabulous.

Jason looked across as if he was reading her mind, and he wasn't one bit amused either. She felt ashamed of her little trick at the show. Cheap, in fact, as if she had been trying to provoke him.

"I could have died when you winked at Jason Tysak at the show," one of her customers said. "Imagine! After all the trouble he's caused you, Tamara. It was quite naughty. Really sexy."

Didn't she just know it? It had seemed like a good idea at the time but now it just seemed to be madness. Jason Tysak was a man to avoid, not provoke.

Roger apparently saw things from another angle.

"You did what?" he muttered as the woman moved away. "You actually winked at Tysak in front of all those people?"

Tamara's cheeks were glowing hot with embarrassment and temper. "It was part of the act and he just happened to be there," she snapped. "And if our friendship is to continue then just back off!"

He turned away and strode out of the room.

Tamara still hadn't got herself under control when a hand came to her elbow and she was ushered firmly to the edge of the bar, where there was a small quiet spot in the middle of turmoil.

"I can see he didn't like it," Jason murmured, handing her another drink.

"Who didn't like what?" she enquired.

"Your boyfriend didn't like the nice, sexy wink," he stated. "I saw him go off raging."

"You're not as observant as I had imagined," Tamara managed. "Roger was annoyed at having to leave. He had a lead to follow up."

"Well, I could see him demanding explanations," Jason murmured. "How did you wriggle out of it?"

"There was nothing to wriggle out of!" Tamara snapped. "The wink was part of the act. You just happened to put your face in the way."

"Really?" He gave her a derisive look. "If young Miss Prost hadn't failed you, as I am informed, would she have delivered the provoking little signal? I can't see her mother allowing that."

"You don't know anything about anything!" Tamara seethed, losing the battle with her blushes.

"I know an invitation when I see one. I also begin to understand that you're not the lovely, bewildered innocent with the unreliable temper I thought you were. State your terms, Tamara, but don't expect to marry a millionaire, will you? It will be just a sleeping partnership."

She tossed her drink right over him and she didn't care who saw. It was all too fast for him to retaliate and she stormed across the room and out into the darkness without looking back. But before she could open the car door, strong hands spun her round as Jason towered over her furiously.

"It's not as easy as that to dispatch me, you little red-haired cat!" he grated.

"Let me go!" Tamara struggled.

"Oh, no," he muttered angrily. "There's action and reaction in everything, and nobody does that to me."

"Nobody speaks like that to me either!" Tamara raged.

"You mean I mistook your intentions?"

He was scathing, looking at her as if she were an awful person, and she had only anger to protect herself.

"Your girlfriend will come looking for you," she spat.

"Let her," he jeered. "She's only a part-time occupation with me and she knows it. Talk is over, Miss
Rawson."

His lips burned into hers, punishing and hard,
stopping her breath, but Tamara just stood there and
accepted it, her body like wood, her mind frozen
against him, the only escape she had.

He lifted his head and looked down at her, seeing
her blank face and the subdued pain in eyes that had
never closed. His own anger seemed to die right then.

"Why did you walk like that, wink like that?
Don't you know what it looked like?"

Tamara was incapable of answering. Suddenly she
just wanted to cry, and his hand softened.

"Oh, Tamara," he murmured. "I'm not going to
hurt you," he assured her softly. He parted her lips
with slow insistence, his hand stroking her face, and
when she began to soften he turned her until he
leaned against the car and she was pulled against his
warmth.

It all began slowly, almost as an apology for Jason's savage attack. Tamara needed comfort and he
was giving it, but before long comfort gave way to
something entirely different as his lips demanded
more and the kiss deepened.

She was shocked when his tongue began to probe
her lips, running along the soft, swollen contours,
and as she gasped his tongue slid inside her mouth,
urgently exploring until she shivered in his arms and
gripped his shoulders desperately. He ran his hand

down her spine, compelling her closer, his legs parting to bring her against him, and she felt the hard arousal of his body for the first time, her own body responding achingly.

His stroking hands discovered the tight, swollen evidence of her breast, and his dark eyes searched her face as his hand slid into the opening of her dress.

"No!" She tried to move away.

"Yes, Tamara," he breathed, taking her lips with his as his hand moved to cover her breast. It was heavy, silken, surging to fill his palm, even though she tried to control the desire that came in a wild rush.

"Please! Please don't," she whispered shakily. "People—"

"Come with me, then," he demanded thickly. 'Leave your car and come home with me. I want you."

"No!" She struggled against him but his arm was like iron. "What will you tell that woman?" she asked bitterly, as his thumb rubbed softly over her nipple.

"The hell with her," he said. "I want *you*."

It brought her back to earth. What was she doing, letting him touch her and make suggestions like that? He was treating her as if she were cheap, willing. He would no doubt say the same thing about her later.

She jerked free violently. "Don't touch me!" she ordered. "Let me get into my car or I'll go back inside and ask for protection."

"Protection? From me?" His expression was stunned.

"I don't know you," she said tightly. "I don't want to know you. You're the enemy."

"Tamara!" He moved towards her but she backed off, staring at him bitterly, and he suddenly turned, his face pale and cold as he walked back towards the party.

She trembled all the way back to her flat, tears of humiliation on her face. Men! How wise she had been to steer clear of them so far. Roger had a chauvinistic chip on his shoulder, and Jason Tysak was a monster! Who did he think he was, acting as if he owned her? For two pins she would start the battle about the mews all over again.

She locked herself in and stood under the shower later, fighting off tears. She tried not to think of the desire that had surged through both of them. It was best forgotten; so was the look in Jason's eyes as he had walked away.

Maybe he wouldn't let them stay now? In four days the leases were due to be signed and she had humiliated him in front of everyone. Nobody knew what he had done to her. She certainly wasn't about to enlighten them either. Once again Jason had won.

The phone rang and she hoped it wasn't Roger. "Hello?" She hadn't expected to put quite so much caution into her enquiry.

"Tamara?" When she didn't answer he spoke even more firmly. "All right. If you don't want to answer

I can understand, but please listen at least. I'm sorry."

It couldn't be Jason apologising? She sat there silently.

"I know perfectly well that the wink was part of the act and I accept that I put my face in the way, as you pointed out. I had no business to speak to you as I did or act as I did. I can only offer the excuse that you have an unfailing ability to infuriate me. It's almost a gift. When I get my hands on you, things seem to slip out of my control."

"I—I'm *not* running after you!" Tamara ventured. "I'm not accustomed to being insulted."

"You retaliated quite perfectly," he assured her. "Would you be interested to know that I have a cherry in my breast pocket?" Tamara felt an attack of the giggles coming on, but she refused to let them. "Next time I'll see you get a lemonade only," he added.

"There won't be a next time," Tamara said. "We're worlds apart, Mr. Tysak, and obviously that's a good arrangement. In all probability we shall never meet again."

"I know," he agreed quietly. "That's why I wanted to apologise. I don't like leaving on a sour note. Goodnight, Tamara. I've enjoyed our clashes. I'll remember you as an unusual opponent. And Tamara, you're beautiful."

He rang off, and it was as if a door had closed in her life. Nothing exciting would happen again in this town after he left, and clearly he was leaving. She wasn't humiliated now. She only remembered the sheer bliss of it, the kisses, his skilled hands. She probably had been too sheltered if she had lived for almost twenty-five years and never felt that before.

The doorbell rang the next morning before Tamara was even dressed. She was shaken to find Jason standing there, looking immaculate. It wasn't raining but there was a lot of heavy cloud, and with the dark background he looked very masculine and virile. He had a grey jacket on with dark trousers and a casual shirt that probably cost a fortune.

"What do you want?" She stared at him solemnly, keenly conscious of her old blue dressing-gown.

"It's Saturday," he pointed out drily.

"I've known other Saturdays. They come each week and I get to sleep late."

"I'm taking you out," he said, and she looked at him warily.

"I'm too much on guard, Mr. Tysak. You've changed my character. And I most certainly do not want to see you again."

"It's all for business. I planned a trip," he assured her.

"I'm glad. Enjoy it. Send me a postcard."

"Tamara!" He looked at her in amused exasperation. "You're keeping me standing on the step. People don't usually treat me like that."

"They'll learn," she muttered, her hand on the door. But before she could stop him he was inside the flat with the door closed, and Tamara turned on him angrily. This was a violation of her rights.

"Go away!" she ordered furiously. "Leave me in peace. I will not discuss business or anything else with you."

"I'm taking you out," he stated flatly. "I want your help and you owe it to me to co-operate. Local concern has been so stirred up that I put a temporary stop on all work—even the hotel—until everything is sorted out. Because of you I'm left with a half-finished hotel and an Edwardian mews I can well do without if it is to sit there unaltered. I need you on my side. Now what do you want for breakfast? I haven't got all day."

"I'll come," Tamara stated mutinously. "But I won't be on your side, not after last night."

"Get dressed!" he ordered fiercely.

In view of his impeccable appearance, Tamara chose her clothes with care. She didn't know what this was all about but she chose mid-blue trousers with a white silk shirt and topped it off with a fine wool jacket of dark biscuit colour.

Even though she was dying to ask where they were going, she desisted, and as they pulled away from her flat in his shining red Jaguar, Tamara sank back into her seat and kept silent.

It turned out to be a hotel in a town some thirty miles north and the Jaguar made short work of the distance. Tamara gazed around her. She had been contemplating coming north to see her mother and father, but it looked very grim at the moment. On this main road there was no flooding, but she could see it across the fields.

"That's not just rain, you know," she said. "A couple of rivers have burst their banks up here, and my mother told me that there's still snow to melt."

"Where do your parents live?" Jason asked.

"Further north by a long way—Cumbria. A little village in the hills. Up there you have to watch the weather."

The hotel was Victorian, beautifully preserved, and there were Victorian shops too. It was a lot like Lancrest Mews but with more shops.

The façades had been beautifully kept, but inside they had been modernised.

Jason took her straight through one shop through a swinging glass door and out into a covered arcade that led straight into the hotel. Even now guests from the hotel were coming into the arcade and straight into the shops. There was no need for them to face the weather outside.

She wandered off by herself, looking in each shop window and thinking about Lancrest Mews. When she walked back Jason was leaning against the hotel doorway, watching her. He had been talking to the manager.

"Let's eat," Jason suggested. "You must be hungry."

She wasn't just hungry—she was stunned into silence. Was this what she had fought to ward off? It was wonderful, and she could see that her custom would grow beyond the people of the town.

The meal had been ordered before she stopped dreaming about it and when she looked at Jason, he was watching her intently.

"Well, Tamara Rawson?" he prompted.

"Is—is this what you intend to do with Lancrest Mews and the Old Manor Hotel?" she gulped.

He simply nodded and went on watching her.

"Did—did you get the idea from here?" she asked.

"No. I've done this sort of thing in several places. Trying to keep traditional things is very important to me. Here, though, there were just the shops and a large adjacent area of waste ground. We built this hotel from old plans, adding modern facilities, of course."

"This is a new hotel?" Tamara couldn't believe it.

"Brand-new," he assured her. "It's been open for about a year and a half and it's always booked up."

"So you own this hotel too?" Tamara asked sombrely.

"This and plenty more," he agreed. "Right now, though, I want to know how you feel about this being repeated in Lancrest Mews."

"It's a wonderful idea," she said almost tearfully. "I'm sorry I fought it but you never stated your case."

"I never got the chance, Tamara," he reminded her. "I offered to show you the plans the first time I saw you but you had some idea that the shop fronts would be plastered into the hotel and left with all the seams showing."

"I didn't understand," Tamara admitted.

"As I recall, it was carved across your heart," he reminded her.

"Sometimes I do things—impulsively," she confessed.

"I know." His voice was suddenly softened and when she looked up his eyes darkened even more. "Do I have a little co-operation in future, with Lancrest Mews?" he asked.

"You can spy for me," he ordered as they ate their meal. "As I see it, this ladies' committee is responsible for a good deal of upheaval."

"I put them up to it," Tamara disclosed worriedly. "I didn't say anything outright, you understand? But I underestimated the power of somebody like Mrs. Prost."

One black eyebrow was raised, but he kept a straight face.

"Never mind," he said quietly. "We'll forget that. Now you're a double agent. I want to know everything they propose to do."

"I couldn't do that, Jason!" Tamara looked shocked.

"You let me know what they were about to do once before," he pointed out. "Just watch out and at least tell me if anything startling is about to happen. Any more and I'll just drop the whole project."

"I'll see what I can do," she promised.

After the meal she wanted to browse through the shops and he had business with the manager, so it was almost dark before they started home.

Initially Tamara was too busy thinking about the future appearance of Lancrest Mews, about Jason, who sat silently and drove, to give much thought to anything else. She wanted time to sort out her feelings for this enigmatic man.

But when he suddenly braked, she came to the present. They were at a bridge but the river had overflowed and the muddy water was sweeping towards them rapidly.

Jason reversed fast and turned the car.

"Sorry, Tamara," he muttered. "Tonight we stay at the hotel. Let's hope they're not full."

She didn't have any misgiving because she somehow knew it was not going to happen. "I don't think we can do it," she said quietly. "I know this area. It's downhill all the way to the hotel in the town, and there's another river about three miles back that might well join forces with this one."

"Are you frightened?" he asked.

"No. Simply pessimistic."

"We'll try for the town anyhow," he said grimly, but they could see the flood water as they topped the last rise.

"Damnation!" Jason snapped. "This is incredible."

"Not really," Tamara stated. "It's wild up here and we've had unprecedented rain. This is the lowest part, so...take to the hills," she ordered.

Four

There was a small road to the side, and Jason obeyed Tamara at once, turning along the narrow road.

"I always keep to the main road when I'm coming home," Tamara said, looking out into the gathering gloom. "I've never been up here, but it seems to me that we have no alternative."

Incredibly, right at the back of beyond there was a village, just a few houses and a tiny inn.

"They won't have accommodation," Tamara stated gloomily.

"We'll see," he said, parking in front.

"You could always walk in and buy the place," Tamara snapped.

"The spoiled-brat syndrome is back, I see," he murmured scathingly. "For a while there I thought you had suddenly grown up, no fuss about the floods, no worry about danger. Now, with rescue in sight, you're back to normal. Wait here," he ordered and she wouldn't have dared do anything else. The parking space was waterlogged.

He was back soon. "They have two rooms. Here we are and here we stay. Out!"

"I haven't any things with me," Tamara complained.

"You'll manage. You look fine without make-up."

"It's not putting it on, it's getting it off!" she argued.

"This is a small place but clean," he assured her. "I imagine that soap will be provided."

Men knew nothing, Tamara decided. She stepped out of the car and water came over her feet, filling her shoes and wetting her trousers.

"This is too much!" she shouted, glaring at Jason.

"Having got wet myself, I'd intended to carry you, but sometimes I get tired of your irritating ways. You'd better follow me closely," he advised. She squelched behind him, filled with hatred. The trousers would clean but the shoes were ruined, and he had done it to put her in her place.

The small inn was cosy, a bright fire burning in the room to the side of the bar. The landlady assured them that they could have a meal, providing they wanted ham and eggs.

"I'll show you to your rooms," she offered, "and then you can come down and have a drink."

Jason went along to his room, still grimly silent, and the landlady stayed chatting to Tamara.

"I hear you're stranded. Not for long, though. By morning you'll get clear because when that river

floods the road it doesn't stay. Too many fields to
fill, you see.''

"Well, it's nice enough here," Tamara assured her,
lying prettily. In fact, it was dismal, the room lit by
one naked bulb overhead and a low-powered bedside lamp. "We haven't anything with us, though,"
she said. "I even got my feet wet."

"Your things will dry by morning. I can let you
have some night things."

Jason was in the bar when she went down, and
they sat by the fire later with their drinks. He seemed
to be in a mood, only replying to Tamara in mono-
syllables.

Later she was obliged to clean her face with soap,
and afterwards she contemplated the nightie on her
bed. It was thick white cotton, two sizes too big but
scrupulously clean, and she put it on.

Trouble came when she went back to the bathroom to clean her teeth. She rubbed vigorously with
her finger and prepared to sneak back to her room.
Jason was probably asleep already in the room next
door.

When she opened the bathroom door the passage
was in total darkness, and then the bathroom light
went off too. Tamara fumed silently, feeling her way
along the wall.

Disaster struck in the form of an old-fashioned
chest, and her bare foot banged into it with some
force. She gave a subdued but angry yelp, clutching

her toe, which had taken the full force of the blow. It was enough to bring tears of pain to her eyes.

The door beside her was wrenched open and Jason towered there, his shirt unbuttoned to the waist.

"What the hell are you doing?" He looked astonished as she stood there on one foot, her other foot clutched in her hand.

"I bumped into this thing. The lights went off." She stood upright, gingerly putting her foot to the ground, an action that brought her directly in line with the lamp that still shone by Jason's bed.

"My overhead light went off too," he said vaguely. "Must be some money-saving device." He moved slowly forward. "What on earth are you wearing?"

"Oh! The landlady lent me this. Didn't you get any pyjamas delivered?"

"Blue striped, a curious size," he murmured, his eyes intently on her. "I don't need any. Old habits..."

"I—er—I'll go, then," Tamara stammered, her face glowing at this admission that he slept naked. "Can you leave your door open until...?"

"I'll see you home," he growled, walking past her to open her door. He went in to light her bedside lamp. "All safe and sound," he added as she hovered at the door. "Just let me look at that foot."

Before she could protest he had her sitting on the bed, her foot in his hand, his long fingers gently probing.

"Your feet are like ice. I must have been out of my mind to let you step into the water."

"It's all right. I'll soon get warm." She was almost whispering, and he stood up quickly, a tight expression on his face.

"Get into bed. I'll close your door on my way out." His voice sounded harsh and she stood, turning away to the bed, her hair hiding her suddenly miserable look. She was as much a nuisance to him as ever.

"Tamara?" She didn't turn. "You look like a child in that astonishing garment. Something out of the past." She refused to look at him even when he turned her and gently tilted her face. "Oh, Tamara," he said softly.

His hand cupped her nape, drawing her forward, pulling her to the hard warmth of his chest. She didn't try to move, didn't try to pretend she wanted to be free, and as he lifted her face she closed her eyes.

"A mixture of fight and submission," he murmured. "Most of the time I could shake the life out of you, and then you look at me with those golden eyes and I want to carry you off."

She opened her eyes then and his face was close, a taut look on it that made her feel weak. When he stared into her eyes she just looked right back until he jerked her forward and covered her lips with his.

It was no gentle kiss. There was the urgent force of necessity, masculine need, demandingly possessive, and the urgency grew as she linked her own slim arms around his neck. His lips parted hers and the kiss deepened to passion as her mouth opened to meet his, and his hands gripped her tightly.

"This is crazy," he murmured, his lips trailing across her hot cheeks. "You know I want you, don't you?" She could only shake her head. "You do!" he said fiercely. "Every time I see you I want to take you to bed right at that moment. It's only when you're out of my sight that sanity returns."

What was he saying—that she was a temptation but unsuitable even as a mistress? Did he think she would willingly...? She gave a little cry and he lifted her right into his arms, looking down at her bewildered face.

"Yes, it's shocking, isn't it? If you come to me you'll be burned like a beautiful moth round a flame. I know it but I still reach for you. Would you come to me, Tamara? Stay with me?" he asked huskily.

She didn't understand his husky words but she would take risks for him. She would risk everything for Jason. She knew it right then, and his lips covered hers as he saw the answer in her eyes.

He lowered her to the bed and came down with her, turning her into his arms, his hands running over her possessively. "You're beautiful," he breathed. "More alluring in this than in that swimsuit even, and God knows I wanted to eat you up then. Now you're demure and trembling."

His lips were trailing over her cheeks, over her throat, his fingers exploring the shell of her ear, and she shivered with a delight she had never felt before at this gentleness. He unfastened the buttons at the front of the nightie, his mouth moving lower, and Tamara moaned with pleasure as his hands cupped her breasts, tight and aroused through the cotton.

"Jason!" She twisted wildly and his hand slid inside, his breathing uneven, and she curled against him.

"It's all right," he murmured thickly, his voice almost unrecognisable. "Nothing is going to hurt you."

His head bent to take the pulsing tip into his mouth, his tongue flicking teasingly against the sharply aware centre, and Tamara arched, trying to escape this ecstasy, but his mouth held her fast, tugging erotically until she reached out and cradled his dark head against her.

"Warm and submissive," he said huskily, his face between her breasts as he stroked her body. "That's how I like you, all that fiery temper turned to desire, and all for me."

He moved over her fiercely, his lips crushing hers, and Tamara suddenly remembered the open door. If anyone walked past . . .

"The—the door..." she whispered, clutching him. He rolled clear and stood, his shoulders tight and controlled in seconds.

"So much for heated moments," he murmured. "Congratulations on keeping your head. Once again, I lost mine." He turned and pulled the sheets aside, covering her as she looked up at him with hurt, bewildered eyes. "You would have been more hurt tomorrow," he stated harshly. "Tomorrow the world begins again. You won't want to remember this."

"I will," she said, a catch in her voice.

"Romance lingers in the air. Only it wasn't romance, Tamara, it was desire, a purely physical need. That's what you should remember."

He strode out of the room, closing the door, and after a while Tamara put out the lamp and lay in the darkness. For the first time in her life she had been willing simply to give herself to a man. Why? Her mind started to tell her but she twisted away from it. She didn't want to know why she was so willing with Jason. But tears were on her cheeks as she fell asleep.

Tamara was awakened early with a cup of tea and a smiling suggestion from the landlady that they would want to be on their way. Her clothes were dry, but her shoes were still very damp and she left them off, padding downstairs to breakfast beside a silent, frowning Jason.

He was no better on the road and Tamara couldn't make idle conversation. Last night was still too much in her mind. As the town came in sight, somehow she knew she would not see him again after this. Everything about him told her that and she wanted to cry very badly.

"Would you mind if I didn't take you to your flat?" he suddenly asked. "I've got a hell of a headache and I can hardly see."

"I'll get a taxi. Drop me off anywhere. Is it a migraine?"

"No," he muttered impatiently. "I expect it's something I've picked up. You'll probably get it too, sorry."

"I'm very healthy. Normally I don't catch things. My dad says—"

"For God's sake, Tamara," he growled. "You'll not get a taxi. You'll take this car. Just drive off when I stumble into my own place."

"I can't take this! It's a Jaguar!"

"But not the variety that bites. It's a metal box with four wheels, like any other car. Go easy on the accelerator and you'll be fine. Now shut up before my head rolls off." Tamara kept quiet until he drew up in front of a large Victorian house with a huge garden and thick hedges.

"Slide over and drive off," he ordered, opening the door. "I'll have it collected later, maybe tomorrow."

"Will you be all right?" She looked up at him anxiously.

"Why? You want to come and tuck me up? I thought you were bright as well as beautiful. Intelligence is the ability to learn."

"I've learned," she said angrily, her face flushing. "Christian charity is caring for anyone who is ill."

"Sweet charity." He looked down at her, his lips quirking, and then he turned wearily to the house. "Mind the damned road," he added vaguely.

"And see if I'll offer to help again," she muttered to herself.

She changed, had a shower and made herself a meal, but even while she was eating it she was wondering what Jason had had to eat, how he was feeling. There was no one to take care of him. That woman he'd been with at the fashion show was back in Paris, he had said. She felt miserable at the thought of any woman, but as the afternoon wore on she kept thinking about him, and at last she collected her coat and bag and went out to the car. It was really asking for trouble but she wouldn't be able to sleep unless she knew he was all right.

Knocking on his door took some courage. There was no bell, just a brass knocker, but no sound came from the darkened house. Jason did not appear.

She searched the key-ring and after two attempts found the door key.

"Jason?" As she stepped into the darkened hall she listened and then called, but there was no answer.

It was a big house, old, and there were plenty of rooms to search, but she skimmed through them. He was upstairs, in the first bedroom she came to, and the sight of him stopped her. He was in bed, deeply asleep, and the sheets had slipped down to expose his bare chest. It suddenly dawned on her that it was freezing in here—the whole house was cold, in fact.

She stood there anxiously for a second, her eyes on him. Even when he was ill, his dark hair damp against his face, he was a disturbing man. There was a sheen of perspiration across his forehead, strands of dark hair falling across it. He moved slightly, stirring in his sleep.

"Jason?" She moved to the bed and spoke his name. His eyes opened a fraction and then closed again.

"Jason!" A wave of near-panic hit her; his eyes had been dazed, the pupils enlarged, and her first thought was to rush out for a doctor. He had only complained of a headache but clearly he couldn't wake up. "*Jason!*"

"Hmm, Tammy." His fingers curled round her arm. "I must be dead—that would explain it."

"Jason! What have you been taking?" She grabbed his hand. "You look drugged."

"Pain-killers!" He glared at her. "Spare me the lecture and get your excuses ready. What the devil are you doing here, sneaking into the house, into my bedroom?"

"I came to bring the car back and there was no light on. I assumed you were collapsed somewhere."

"I told you the car would be collected," he rasped, "but, even if I hadn't, does that give you the right to come in?"

"I'll ignore the fact that you're a hateful and beastly human being," Tamara snapped. "Normal people worry about each other, but then, you wouldn't know that."

"Back to sweet charity, are we?" he growled. He slid down in the bed, closing his eyes. "Get out of here, Tamara."

He slid further down, pulling the sheets up to his ears.

"You need something to eat," Tamara began firmly, but this time he roared at her.

"Out, Tamara! If you're there two seconds from now I'll get up and put you out myself." Since he was wearing exactly nothing, the threat had the desired effect and she went quickly. He needed help but he was too pig-headed to accept it. He needed a doctor, a hot drink, something to eat, and the boiler wanted lighting.

The doctor was her first call and he took a bit of persuading.

"I'm your doctor, Tamara, not Tysak's," he protested.

"He hasn't got a doctor," she pleaded. "He looks really ill. I'm quite worried."

Dr. Harrison and her father had been at medical school together and kept in touch; that was why she had chosen him.

"What are you doing there anyhow?" he asked.

"It's a long story," Tamara said uneasily. "Er—"

"Never mind. It sounds as though it will take some time to concoct an excuse. I'll be on my way—but mark this down as a favour to you, my girl. I only attend the really sick on Sundays."

"He really is ill," she assured him.

"We'll see."

She stifled her annoyance and turned her mind to the boiler. It looked like a dangerous old relic, but she found the pilot-light and twelve matches later, she had the satisfaction of seeing it burn steadily.

When Dr. Harrison came Tamara pointed him in the right direction and then stayed out of the firing line. Then, hearing him coming down the stairs she went to meet him and drew him into the kitchen.

"How is he?" Her eyes were wide with concern.

"He'll live. I should know better, shouldn't I?" he enquired. "I've known you since you were a little girl and you've not altered much. This time, however, you can't control the situation. Tysak has a mind of his own."

"I only acted because he was ill, and when a friend—"

"What friend are we talking about? I know all about the battle between you and Tysak with those daunting ladies who back you like a flotilla of ships."

"It's not like that now," she said hurriedly. "We've got a business arrangement. Yesterday we had a business trip and that's how I knew he was ill."

"Quite!" He looked at her suspiciously. "Anyway, he's got a bug. It's going round and he did everything right. No need for me. He took pain-killers and went to bed. It's damned cold in here!" he added, glancing round.

"It's all right. I've lit the boiler. Now what shall I give him to eat?"

"Hot soup if he can take it. Plenty to drink." He looked down at her sternly. "You can't stay here, Tamara."

"He's perfectly civilised!" she protested, lying vigorously. He was anything but civilised.

"You shouldn't be here, Tamara," he insisted. "Your father wouldn't like it."

"I'll just make him some soup and then I'm going back to my flat. I've got work to do tomorrow. Two busy days after the show, and then it's Easter. I'll be going home."

"Good. You should stay clear of Jason Tysak. You're a babe in arms at the side of somebody like that. Give my regards to Jeffrey and Susan." He smiled.

"I've brought you some soup," Tamara informed Jason briskly, a little while later, avoiding the dark eyes that followed her progress across the room. "I got the boiler going. I called the doctor, heated a tin of soup and that lets me out."

"You fiddled about with that dangerous contraption?" He pulled himself up in bed to glare at her.

"Pretty soon it will be warmed up. I'll come back when you've had this and leave you a drink before I go."

"What makes you think I won't drag you into bed with me?"

Tamara fled and she was not amused when she heard that low dark laughter again. He was so hateful! All the same, when she went back in with a stiff, angry face he was lying down, already back into the half-drugged sleep. He looked ill. She put the drink by his bed.

"Thanks, Tamara," he muttered sleepily. "The soup was welcome and I'm warm now. I appreciate your help. Now go away, there's a good girl. I'll live."

It was while she was getting the key into the door of the Jaguar that another car slowed down opposite. She glanced up, and froze into near horror at the sight of Mrs. Prost eyeing her oddly before driving off. That had *really* let the cat out of the bag!

As usual, the rush of trade after the fashion show was enormous, and they were kept at it all the next morning. Janet went out to get some sandwiches for them both, and while she was out Jason phoned.

"I'm alive," he volunteered.

"I'm so glad. We're very busy and I expect I'll be late tonight. Could you arrange for your car to be collected, do you think? It's parked outside my flat."

"Who's going to care for me?" he asked. "Suppose I fall down the stairs?"

"I think you'll survive. In any case, I'll have to go now," she added as Janet came in.

"Wait! It's utterly miserable being here alone."

"How self-pitying. Just like a man," she jeered. "Anyway, I don't like the house."

"I'll sell it. Come and make dinner for me."

"I'm not promising." She knew her cheeks were glowing.

"If you don't, I'll get up and come round to your flat."

"Jason!" Her little cry was lost on him.

"I'm missing you," he said and put the phone down.

Mrs. Prost came in straight after lunch and looked down her nose somewhat at Tamara.

"Surely I saw you in our part of town last evening?" she asked sharply.

"Yes," Tamara said. "When somebody is ill I'm afraid I can't ignore it."

"Jason Tysak? Weren't you driving his car?"

"I was." Tamara bit back the urge to tell her to mind her own business. "I'll be taking it back tonight too," she added. "I promised to make him a meal. Dr. Harrison thinks he should take care for a couple of days."

"I'm surprised you were the one to offer your help," Mrs. Prost said bleakly. "He's caused you a lot of trouble."

"I caused the trouble, Mrs. Prost," Tamara said determinedly. "The plans that Jason has for Lancrest Mews are really wonderful. You'll be well pleased. We went to see a place just like it on Saturday. I was most impressed."

"You went with *him*? The rumours are true, then? I'm quite shocked. Staying to take care of him will not do any good for your reputation either."

"It's called Christian charity, Mrs. Prost! Try it!" Tamara snapped.

"Is it? And what was it to that other woman who was staying there? I wonder what kind of charity that was?"

She didn't wait for an answer, and the way the door slammed shut told Tamara that she had lost a customer. But all she could hear was the poisonous remark about the other woman. She should have been grateful, since it was true, however bitchily said. She needed reminding.

When they finally got the shop closed she went back to her flat and rang Jason.

"I can't come," she said straight away.

"It doesn't matter," he said heavily. "I'll just sleep."

"Are you worse?" Caution left her at the sound of his voice. He seemed to be weary, ill.

"I couldn't eat a thing." He just put the phone down. What was she to do now?

"Back to the Jaguar," she muttered, and on the way there she collected things for dinner, parking

Jason's car in the High Street with a "Devil take them all" attitude that lived deep in her character. They were going to talk anyway, so let them. The stab of pain when the woman from Paris had been mentioned had told her what she had known for some time. She loved Jason.

When she went up the stairs to his room he was leaning back against the pillows, his eyes on the door.

"So you came after all?"

"You didn't sound too good on the phone. I changed my mind."

"I'm never *good*, Tamara," he taunted. "Surely you know that?"

"It's none of my business," she said briskly, and walked out before he could say any more. It wouldn't take long to make a meal because she had cheated and bought quite a few ready-made things.

When she looked up he was leaning in the doorway, watching her. He had dressed in casual clothes, grey trousers and a black sweater, and she just stared at him.

"Should you be up?"

"Probably not, but all the same I'm here." He walked across and sat at the kitchen table. "Can I have a drink?"

"Water or tea?"

"No use asking for a whisky, I expect?"

"None whatever. You know perfectly well that with those tablets you shouldn't have alcohol."

"Tea?" he enquired with such meekness that she shot him a suspicious look before she broke off to make it.

They stayed where they were for the meal. Every time she looked up Jason's eyes met hers, and, although his looks taunted, she could see perfectly well that he should not be out of bed at all.

It was not until she walked past him to the dishwasher that she made any mistakes at all. She passed too close and he grabbed her, pulling her down on to his knee.

"Now, then, Miss Trouble," he said sternly. "Why did you refuse to come after I begged so humbly? Why did you change your mind? And what's this silence about?"

"I—I shouldn't be here, sitting here . . ."

"Possibly not, but I'm enjoying it."

"Mrs. Prost saw me leave last night," she said stiffly.

"Ah! The champion gossip. And then what?"

"She came to the shop to pry and ended up remonstrating with me," Tamara said quietly.

"I imagine you had a good excuse ready?" he enquired.

"I did not! Why should I wriggle about, lying to her? I snapped at her and she left haughtily."

"So, little wild-cat, you lost a good customer? You realise she'll spread it all around town?

"She'd better be careful what she says!"

"I think she will be," he assured her, "especially if she mentions it to her husband first. You see, I've opened an account at his bank and I'm sorry to say that managers tend to drool a bit over a Tysak account."

"Why—why have you...?" She had a sudden burst of hope that he really intended to stay here.

"I'm not sinking the firm's money into the town," he said drily. "Just some of my personal account."

His hand was warm against her face, his eyes running over the creamy satin of her skin and she could see desire beginning to flare in his gaze.

Tamara jumped up, moving rapidly away from him. She ignored the flash of emotion that crossed his face. She had emotions too, and Jason had turned her world upside-down.

"Are you scared to look at me?" he asked softly when she kept her face turned away.

"I'm not particularly scared of anyone." It was a bit tricky to keep control of her voice. "Did I tell you that we're closing down early for Easter?"

"And then what?"

She kept her head down, rubbing at the sink. "I go home. I'll be back the Wednesday after Easter."

"You'll be away for a week." He sounded weary again.

"Good reckoning. One whole week of bliss, nothing but country air and home cooking. I expect we'll have a houseful of relatives over Easter. It usually—"

"Tamara! Shut up!"

Jason sounded almost violent and she stopped at once, not a bit surprised when he got up and left the room.

Five

Jason wasn't in bed when she went cautiously to his room. He was standing by the window, just staring out into the darkness. He was still dressed, and as she went in he turned.

"Not gone yet?" He sounded bleak.

"Just going. Here's your drink. I'll put it near the bed." She moved quickly to the bedside table, her face once again turned away. "I wish you would get somebody to collect your car," she got out a bit desperately. "I'll be packing tomorrow night and then the flat will be empty for a week. I—I'm not sure if it will be safe just left there."

She had no idea he had moved until his hand came to her shoulder, moving upwards to brush her hair aside and expose the tender nape. His lips brushed her neck beneath the red-gold shine of hair.

"There's no need to talk so frantically," he murmured, his lips against her skin. "I know you're scared. You've hardly stopped trembling since we first met." He turned her slowly, looking down at her when she refused to meet his gaze. "You're sensible, too, running home to Mother and that safe family."

"I'm not running!" She looked up to protest and met dark eyes that were vibrant with feeling. "It's Easter."

"Take care, then," he warned. "Avoid floods and small hotels."

"I will." She moved away, filled with bitter pain when he let her go readily. She didn't want to look at him again in case she cried.

"Tammy!" His voice stopped her when she was no more than a step away from him, and at the warm sound of that little change to her name she turned back.

"Going home is the most sensible thing you could do," he said in a stilted voice. "If you go I'll know it's for the best and I'll go too. The project doesn't need me. It will just go on. You'll be sensible and I'll be wise." His eyes ran over her face, seeing the unshed tears, and he reached out for her. "But I don't want to be wise. Stay with me, Tamara! Oh, God, I need you!"

He buried his face in the warmth of her neck and she clung to him as she had wanted to do so often, so filled with tearful happiness that talking was impossible.

"I want you and I can't fight it any longer. I want to make love to you, sleep with you in my arms, feel your skin against mine. Stay with me!"

She was trembling too much to answer. Her lips sought his blindly and he crushed her to him, his mouth opening over hers, demanding, devouring, a wild rush of passion that left her weak. Molten feeling ran through her as his hands caressed her urgently and she knew that, whatever happened now, the rest of her life would be filled with the wonder of this moment.

There was passion in Jason that she felt like a storm, his hands impatient as they moved over her, finding the soft surge of her breasts and grasping them through the fine wool of her sweater. He pulled the garment over her head, tossing it down with his own and propelling her back into his arms. Moans of pleasure mingled in their warm breath as their skin met for the first time, and Tamara clung to him, lifting her face to his.

Jason's lips devoured her, his hands on her breasts, his thumbs rubbing erotically over the darkened nipples until she sagged against him, every bone melting.

"Come to me, Tammy," he demanded deeply, his lips trailing like fire over her skin. "Melt into me, need me!" His teeth fastened on her ear, biting at the tender lobe as his fingers moved to the zip of her jeans, propelling it down so that they just clung to her hips. It gave him access to her skin and his hands slid inside the waistband, finding the warmth, slowly caressing the rounded length of her thighs.

It was something she had never known, this feeling of being completely taken over, a brilliantly soaring excitement growing inside her that drove all caution away. She moved against him, her actions purely instinctive, rhythmical, until he growled low in his throat and sank his mouth against her neck with hungry pressure.

Tamara cried out. She wanted to be part of him, her mind utterly bewitched, and her hands sought the smooth skin of his back, moving over it, exploring, urging him closer until the coiled passion inside him snapped and his mouth came back to crush hers, his tongue forcing itself between her lips. She was so given up to feeling that nothing else entered her mind, not the thought of the end of this or the thought that Jason accepted her actions as if she were accustomed to a lover.

The sudden, strong, pulsing movement of his tongue excited her more, made her shake with desire, as he moved her to strip off her clothes, and she lay exactly where he put her on the bed, her eyes closed, her body tossing in torment as he undressed, his dark eyes burning down.

She felt him move close and her hands reached out for him, his name a frenzied whisper in her throat.

"Soon, darling. Very soon," he promised thickly and her hands sank into the thick darkness of his hair as he bent to caress every part of her slender shape. Her restless movements brought further heat to him, but when his hand slid between her thighs and his head bent lower to join it she cried out in shocked protest.

"No! Jason, please!"

"Yes! Relax, darling. Enjoy everything." His persistent caresses brought sobs to her throat. She had not given any thought to this, had not even imagined it. She was overwhelmed at her own innocence, ashamed to be so inexperienced.

"Please, Jason! I've never . . . I don't know what to do."

He lifted his head and looked up at her, his eyes like flame and his body quite still.

"Tamara?" He sounded stunned. "You're a virgin? I'm the first man who ever did this to you, held you like this?"

"I—I'm sorry . . ."

"Sorry?" His eyes swept over her. "God help me, I'm not sorry. I want it to be me. The thought of any other man touching you is enough to drive me insane."

Now there was tenderness that cloaked his fierce desire and her limbs melted, relaxed while heat flooded every part of her as he went back to his persistent caressing.

When he moved to lie covering her, his hands moulding her breasts, she clutched him tightly, her body moving to accommodate him as he moved against her demandingly.

"Now ask me to love you, Tammy. It's what I want to hear."

"Please, Jason!" She arched against him wildly, spasms already starting deep inside her, wanting something she could only imagine but wanting it urgently.

He moved against her fiercely, his weight a wonderful burden as his lips cut off her wild cry of pain and passion at the strong thrust of his desire. "Tammy!" He held her fast, his face against her burning cheeks. "Relax, darling. I've got you safe. It's all right."

The burst of pain passed as if it had never been and she gasped as he began to move inside her, her woman's body joining the rhythm, her arms tightening until their lips fused together and release came in a swirl of gold and silver stars and black, velvet oblivion.

When she managed to open her eyes he was leaning over her, watching her, and she suddenly realised there were tears on her face, tears he was quite aware of. She lifted her fingers to brush them away, but he tilted her head, gathering the tears with his lips.

"I—I didn't expect to cry," she whispered.

"If you hadn't I would have been disappointed," he murmured, his lips trailing over her cheeks. "I would have known that the feeling didn't go deep enough." His eyes held hers. "You gave me everything, Tammy, not just your lovely body, but something from deep inside you. That's never happened to me before."

She didn't understand.

"Didn't you like it?" she asked.

"Like it? I'll never be alive again," he said softly. "I've been thrown out of heaven. Go to sleep now. It will be morning all too soon."

She woke up late, instantly aware of her surroundings, deliriously happy to find Jason there beside her. It was like being singingly alive for the first time.

She wanted to wake him up, talk to him, but there was the shop. There was so much to do, and now she wouldn't go home, unless Jason went with her. She wanted to welcome him into the safety of her family, to let him feel the love, but he would have to decide that.

She dressed quickly and silently, creeping from the room. She would make breakfast for him before she went. She would only wake him then. Maybe she would come back at lunchtime to talk.

When somebody knocked on the door she raced to it, wondering if it was the post. It must be a parcel, she decided.

It was not the post, and Tamara's world seemed to shatter as she saw the woman who stood there. She had come back from Paris, this woman who stayed with Jason.

"Hello? You look familiar." She just walked in as if she lived there, and Tamara backed away in the face of such assurance. "Ah! Now I've got it! You're the girl from the fashion show. The one who infuriated Jason. Have you been making it up with him, then?''

''He's ill. I—I just popped in to see if he wanted anything but I don't think he's up yet.'' It was astonishing how speedily the mind prepared a defence. ''As you're here, you'll want to take over.''

''I'm Claire Devereux, by the way. What's wrong with him? I was banking on taking him back with me today.''

''Well, I—I'm sorry. He's got a bug. It's going round. And I'm late. Must go.''

Tamara retreated, snatching up her things.

''I suppose I'd better go up and see to him,'' Claire said unwillingly. ''Thank you. It was good of you to help him, Miss . . . ?''

''Rawson, Tamara Rawson.''

She almost ran out of the door, shutting it behind her and going blindly down the path, her mind not really working.

Over and over she glanced at her watch, ashamed when she realised she had been waiting for him to ring. She had wanted him to call and say that Claire meant nothing to him, but by now he might even be on his way to Paris. He had been well enough to make love to her the night before—passionately.

Tamara's cheeks burned at the memory and she bit into her lips hard to stop tears coming. If only this day would end. If only she could get away.

"I really think we're being boycotted!" Janet said with annoyance as lunchtime approached and the trickle of custom became even thinner.

"Do you think Mrs. Prost...?"

"I certainly do!" Janet muttered. "That woman got brought down to size. She's been round her cronies and spread the word, believe me. I know that lot. I've lived in this town all my life."

"Maybe I should learn to hold my tongue," Tamara mused, but Janet scoffed that to oblivion.

"Why should you? She's an interfering busybody."

"And we're almost empty." Tamara sighed.

"They'll be back!" Janet stated. "And then we'll have the upper hand and we'll not lose it again. We'll condescend a bit, like all high-class shops."

Tamara smiled for the first time that day.

"You're a great tonic," she admitted. "How would you feel if I went off now? I'm going home tomorrow and I've got a lot to do."

"Get off now," Janet urged. "Nothing seems to be happening here and if it suddenly does, I can cope. Go on! It's a long way to Cumbria."

"Shall we try to eat lunch outside?" Susan Rawson smiled at Tamara and the young man who sat beside her.

"Worried about having me back indoors, Aunt Sue?" Robbie Breck turned his teasing blue eyes on his aunt.

"Of course!" Tamara's mother retorted, well used to his ways. "Well, what do you think, Tamara?"

"It's unexpectedly warm," Tamara agreed. "Let's chance it."

"Pneumonia notwithstanding," Robbie murmured as his aunt went inside. "Isn't she wonderful, Tam? I don't get here nearly so often now, what with the business and all."

Tamara smiled across at him. It was good to have Rob here. "How's the business?" she asked, leaning back in the garden chair.

"Good. Very good," he conceded.

"How can a firm that makes mock-antiques do so well?"

"*Mock*? Wretched female! These are the antiques of tomorrow. I don't go round copying things!"

"I know, but it's only sort of crafty woodwork, isn't it?" Tamara teased her much loved cousin.

"Crafty woodwork?" He sprang up at her and Tamara raced for the safety of the apple tree with Rob behind.

He swung her round, but her shrieks of laughter were stilled as her mother came to the door.

"Do try to be civilised, you two," she chided. "Tamara has a visitor."

Tamara had already seen the tall dark man who stood beside her mother. Jason's eyes were on both of them.

"I'm interrupting," he said politely. "I should have let you know."

"You're not interrupting," Rob informed him cheerfully. "You've just saved Tam from injury."

"I'll get some tea for you all," Susan Rawson said. "It's at least half an hour to lunch. Of course you'll stay, Mr. Tysak?" She didn't wait for an answer and after another quick look at Jason, Rob shot off into the house, muttering that he would help. It left Tamara facing Jason.

"I've brought the lease for you to sign," he said tightly. "The others have signed theirs."

"I could have signed it after Easter," Tamara said. "There was no need for you to go to all this trouble."

"I want everything wrapped up before I go away." There was no sign of a smile, no sign that he even remembered the other night. Tamara risked a quick glance at him.

"I see." She looked down at her hands.

"Do you?" he rasped. She was saved by the arrival of her mother and Rob with the tea-tray.

"J-Jason has brought me the lease to sign," she said brightly.

"Well, that's nice. Everything's settled, then." Her mother beamed and Jason smiled his tight smile.

"Completely settled," he stated harshly. He was dangerous again, a savage just below the skin, his dark eyes like menacing pools. Rob's teasing chatter stopped and he glanced at Tamara, then winked soothingly when he saw her anxiety. Unfortunately Jason saw it too and stood up.

"I'm sorry," he said politely to her mother. "I have very little time and I must talk to Tamara."

"Of course. Why don't you go for a walk by the wood, darling?" she said to Tamara. "You can talk—er—business there and work up an appetite for lunch."

Tamara nodded and smiled weakly, and Jason took her arm in a deceptively calm grip.

She moved her arm out of his grip when the house was no longer in sight.

"I'm sorry I interrupted your time with Rob," he said harshly. "Obviously I had no idea you had someone tucked away up here. I can see why you shot off so quickly." It dawned then, and Tamara's golden eyes opened wide.

"Robbie is my cousin!" she snapped. "Even if he weren't, it would surely be none of your business. I didn't enquire about Claire!"

It seemed to make him even more annoyed, and he grabbed her arms.

"Claire is my sister!" he grated.

"You said she was a part-time occupation. You implied that—"

She is," he muttered furiously, "one I could well do without. She divorced Devereux, but wants to go back. I escort her back and within days she's quarrelling again and racing to England and me. When I move I'm keeping my address secret."

"Why did you let me believe . . . ?" she began.

"Because I wanted to keep you out of my life," he told her tightly. "But you walked into my path, Tamara, and you kept on coming. I still can't handle it, so I'm tying up the loose ends and moving on."

"I'm a—a loose end?" Tamara asked, fighting tears.

"Oh, yes," he said quietly, "the biggest one there is. That's why I'll not be coming back. Believe me, it's better for both of us." He turned away, his jaw tight. "I'm in love with you, Tamara."

It hit her like an arrow, deep inside, a shaft of beautiful feeling that made her legs weak. He loved her!

"I—I don't understand..." she began shakily. "Don't you want to—to love me?" Her hand came to his arm almost timidly and he looked down at her slender fingers.

"No. I don't want to love you, Tamara. You need marriage, children, a warm family, but not from me. I'm almost thirty-seven."

"What has that to do with it? I'm nearly twenty-five."

"I will never marry," Jason interrupted. "I've seen marriage—my parents, my sister. I know what happens to children when a marriage breaks up. I've experienced it, too. That's not for me."

"How can you say that the same will happen if—?"

"One day you'll meet someone of your own enchanting age," he said wearily. He turned and saw the tears in her eyes. "Oh, Tammy. I wanted you so much. I couldn't resist you in the end and you gave me everything." He grimaced ruefully. "Oh, I could live with you, but I wouldn't even ask you. You're not like me." He looked round, across the hills. "All this. This is you. Family, affection, more than all my wealth. One day you'd leave me. I just couldn't face it."

"I wouldn't leave you, Jason," she said softly.

"Now perhaps you think not. You'll change, Tamara. You'll change and grow. I will never change."

"If you loved me you'd want to stay, want to be with me. Excuses! You didn't phone me. I just walked out of your house while you were still asleep, but you didn't wonder why. Stop lying to me! You were glad to see me go. It lets you off the hook."

He turned eyes on her that were almost fire but stopped when he saw tears streaming down her cheeks.

"I thought you'd simply gone to work," he explained tightly. "I woke up and Claire was there, complaining, demanding. My head was killing me too. When I phoned the shop you'd left. Janet only knew the name of this village. I searched for you, Tamara," he ended wearily.

"If—if you searched for me...why did you bother? Why didn't you just go away and forget it all? You don't trust me. You don't trust anyone."

"I'll always hurt you, Tamara," he said sombrely. "Everything about me will hurt you. If I stay we'll go on being lovers and you know it. That's not for you."

By the time they got back to the house Tamara was in control of her feelings, and it helped that she was numb with disbelief. She loved him. He said he loved her but he was ruthlessly cutting her out of his life.

Two weeks later Tamara stood in the shop as Mrs. Prost left with one of the season's most expensive suits.

"I won't say I told you so," Janet murmured as the door closed. "Notice the change of attitude?"

"Do you think we have the upper hand?" Tamara asked.

"Oh, yes." Janet smiled quite smugly. "They've noted our superior attitude too. We'll not have any trouble in future."

Tamara turned away. It was true that Janet had adopted an attitude that had impressed. She, however, had not needed to. She just wasn't interested any more.

Before she'd left home she had told her mother about Jason. In fact, she hadn't been able to avoid it because after he went she had broken down and shut herself away to weep. Inside she knew that if he really loved her he would be here now, but she hadn't seen him again.

She had stuck it out for a whole week and then driven past his house. Outside was an estate agent's board. For Sale. He had gone.

His office confirmed that Mr. Tysak was in London for one day more and then he would be in America. He wasn't coming back. The business at this end was completed.

So it seemed, completed or abandoned. Nobody was working on the hotel, everything had settled into limbo and Tamara suspected he would finally sell everything.

She was just finishing her supper when Roger called at the flat. Over the two weeks they had made up their differences. He had accepted that friendship was all he was going to get.

"I wasn't expecting visitors," she told him, looking down at her dressing-gown. "I'm having a lazy evening."

"I'm not staying long." Roger closed the door. "Let's have a cup of tea. I've got something to tell you. As a matter of fact, I need advice."

It was all explained as they drank their tea.

"I've been offered a job on a big London paper," Roger told her. "Actually, I applied in a fit of temper, the night after the fashion show and our big row. I never thought about being accepted."

"So what's the problem? Will you be the editor?"

He laughed uproariously.

"No way, love! I'm a newsman from the backwoods. It's only because I'm the editor of the local rag that I've made it at all. The job is for features editor."

"Is that good?" Tamara asked ingenuously.

"It's good. Should I take it, though?" He looked at her. "If I thought for one moment that you—"

"I'm your friend, Roger. Nothing more. If you want this job then go for it."

"Tysak left, Tamara," he said grimly.

"I know. I don't expect to see him again."

"The hotel is going ahead, and the work on Lancrest Mews. Did you know it?" he asked.

"No, but I'm glad. It will be really good. I saw something like it when Jason and I went...went..."

"Oh, Tamara!" He took her hand but she moved away, and began walking about.

"It's all right. Let's talk about this job of yours."

They talked for an hour, and by the time he left he was convinced.

The bell rang soon after and she got up, glancing round. As far as she could see, Roger hadn't left anything behind. Maybe in the hall.

When she opened the door, Jason stood there, tall, dark, looking at her with blazing eyes. He just came right in, and she stepped back, speechless.

"I can see that you're different," he rasped, his eyes running over her. "As I understand it, you never used to float around in your robe when Hart was here. Are you back with him?"

"What do you want? Why are you here?" She just stared at him.

"Answer my question! What was Hart doing here?"

"It comes under the heading of none of your business," Tamara said. "You have no right even to come here, Jason."

"I want to have the right," he said in a desperate voice. "These two weeks have been hell. I had to come back."

Tamara turned slowly to look at him. It was a bit too early to let her guard down and she knew it. Anyone with any sense would make him state his intentions quite clearly, but somehow she knew she would never have that sort of sense with Jason. He would always be the driving force in her life.

"Tamara, I just know that I love you and I can't walk out of your life. You're too much a part of mine."

He swept her up into his arms and walked through to the sitting-room, holding her, and Tamara clung to him tightly, hardly able to breathe. He sat down and held her on his knee, his hand cupping her flushed face.

"Tammy, darling!" He began to kiss her, giving her no time to say anything at all. "I had to come back to you. If you finally leave me it's a chance I'll have to take. I suppose everyone takes that chance when they get married."

"Are you asking me to marry you?" Tamara wanted to know, great joy bubbling up inside.

"I'm telling you," he assured her grimly. "I won't take no for an answer either."

She pulled back and smiled up into his face.

"You won't get no for an answer. And I'll never leave you, Jason. I'll be that immovable object always."

He gave a shaken laugh and began to kiss the silken line of her throat.

"I've thought it all out," he whispered. "I'll have you so tied up in my life that getting free would be impossible. You'll have too many children. You'll be too busy."

"I want children," Tamara said dreamily, lying back in his arms. "We'll be surrounded by love and warmth."

He slid down the zip of her robe and found the warm curve of her breast.

"Go on," he urged huskily. "I can listen to this all night." But when he carried her to the lamplit bedroom she melted into his arms.

"I could stand to hear three little words," Jason murmured against her skin when at last their breathing returned to normal. "Tell me, sweetheart, even if you only say it once in your life."

"I'll never stop saying it," Tamara cried, raining hot kisses against his face. "I love you, Jason. I've fought you but I suppose I've loved you from the moment I saw you."

"I *wanted* you from the moment I saw you," he confessed wryly, smiling at her. "Tammy, say you'll never leave me!"

"Never, ever," she promised softly, her hands cupping his face. "I've got a very stable home background."

"I sold my house. You didn't like it anyway, and neither did I. We could buy a place pretty close to your mother and father—if you want that?"

"Oh, Jason, I do!" Her hands reached out for him. "I want to draw you so closely into my life that you'll never even think of life without me."

"Just so that our house is filled with my children, starting very soon."

"Geronimo," Tamara muttered, blushing prettily.

"I never did find out why you said that when we first met," he murmured.

"I thought you were a noble savage," Tamara said. "I felt like a demure maiden, ordained to serve you."

"*You*?" He gave a great shout of laughter. "My beautiful darling, you lie as wonderfully as you do everything else. I'll spend the rest of my life watching my step and I know it."

"Behind every powerful man is a good woman," Tamara said.

"I almost forgot," Jason murmured as they sat side by side in the sitting-room later. "You had a birthday." He slipped a glittering ring on to her finger as she watched, enchanted. "Engaged!" he stated firmly. "Mine!"

Tamara twisted her hand, watching the diamonds glitter.

"I suppose this is how you get to be really rich," she sighed. "A birthday and engagement rolled into one."

"Well, I thought about it," Jason laughed, "but I felt I could afford a present. How about these?" He presented her with earrings to match the ring. "That covers just about everything," he said softly.

"So what's left?" Tamara asked, her cheeks flushing at the look in his eyes.

"The family," he decided, pulling her close. "We should get around to that at once, and no arguments."

"Not one," Tamara agreed, winding her arms around his neck.